A King Production presents…

D1593026

A Titillating Tale

A Novelette

JOY DEJA KING

This novelette is a work of fiction. Any references to real people, events, establishments, or locales are intended only to give the fiction a sense of reality and authenticity. Other names, characters, and incidents occurring in the work are either the product of the author's imagination or are used fictitiously, as those fictionalized events and incidents that involve real persons. Any character that happens to share the name of a person who is an acquaintance of the author, past or present, is purely coincidental and is in no way intended to be an actual account involving that person.

ISBN 10: 1-942217-81-1
ISBN 13: 978-1942217817
Cover concept by Joy Deja King
Cover model: Joy Deja King

Library of Congress Cataloging-in-Publication Data;
A King Production
Toxic...A Titillating Tale by Joy Deja King
For complete Library of Congress Copyright info visit;
www.joydejaking.com
Twitter @joydejaking

A King Production
P.O. Box 912, Collierville, TN 38027
A King Production and the above portrayal log are trademarks of A King Production LLC

This Novelette is Dedicated To My:

Family, Readers, and Supporters.
I LOVE you guys so much. Please believe that!!

—Joy Deja King

"Gotta argue with him 'cause a nigga love
a toxic bitch..."

~Cardi B~

A KING PRODUCTION

Toxic...

A Titillating Tale

A Novelette

JOY DEJA KING

Chapter One

LOVE HATE

Got Time Today

"Look at that trifling nigga right there," Harper seethed. "He about to make me fuck my nails up." She glanced down at her freshly done, blush pink mountain peak nails with rhinestone swirls, as her fury continuied to simmer.

"Girl, let's just go. You don't need this drama. You got plenty of other options. You won't have no problem replacing him. Fuck Jamari!" Taliyah was doing her best to get her friend to leave the scene, but it wasn't working. When Harper got amped up, there was nothing nobody could do to lower her temperature.

"Nah, fuck that." Harper's tone had turned calm but icy, which only meant she was about to raise hell. "He ain't about to play me out here in these streets." She grabbed her purse and quickly jumped out her car with Taliyah trailing behind her.

Amina make me so sick! Why the hell did she have to call Harper and let her know Jamari was up in Phipps Plaza shopping wit' the next chick, Taliyah thought to herself as she watched Harper approach her boyfriend.

"What's good?!" Harper popped, sounding more like a dude than the prissy princess her outer appearance exuded. It was the main reason she always had problems with men. They thought they would be dating some submissive eye candy. By the time they realized she had the mindset of a nigga, who just so happened to look good in a dress, it was too late.

"Baby, what you doing here?" Jamari asked nervously, as he was putting shopping bags in the trunk of his car.

"I see you did some shopping. What you buy me?" Harper questioned, grabbing one of the Louis Vuitton bags.

"Umm, that's mine!" The chick with Jamari shouted trying to snatch the bag out Harper's hand.

"I advise you to let go of this bag, and stay the fuck outta this. This between me and Jamari. You don't want this smoke....I promise you," Harper warned.

The girl didn't know anything about Harper, but her instincts told her the bitch was crazy. So she stepped back, and directed her attention back to the man who had just taken her on a shopping spree. Her first one at that. She didn't want to mess things up with him, but she wasn't trying to scrap in the mall parking lot either.

"Jamari, what's going on... and who is she?" the girl smacked, folding her arms with an attitude.

"Yeah Jamari, who am I?" Harper smirked, enjoying how rattled he was. Although he was trying to act like he had everything under control, his eyes were telling a different story.

"Baby, let me speak to you for a minute." Jamari spoke smoothly, reaching out his hand, and gently taking Harper's arm.

"Get tha fuck off me!" She barked, yanking her arms out his grasp, before pulling out her baby Glock, that she never left home without.

"Yo, yo, yo!" Jamari put his hands up, slowly stepping back.

"I knew that bitch was crazy," the girl who was with Jamari mumbled, shaking her head. Her first thought was to get her phone and call the police, but quickly realized she had already put her purse in the car. She didn't want to draw unwanted attention to herself by opening the passenger door, so she remained in the background quiet.

"Harper, put the gun away and let's go," Taliyah sighed. She was used to her friend's antics but the shit was draining.

"You can go wait in the car for me, 'cause I got time today. We ain't done here, but this won't take much longer," Harper told her friend, keeping her gun aimed at Jamari.

"Baby, please calm down," Jamari pleaded, keeping his hands up. "It's not what you think. You know I love you."

"You so full of shit," Harper laughed wickedly. "It's always you pretty boys that think you can sweet talk yo' way out some lies."

Harper continued to laugh as she began grabbing the pricey items out of the shopping bags. One-by-one, she tossed them in the mud puddles that hadn't dried up from the storm the night before.

"No you fuckin' didn't!" The girl with Jamari screamed. Horrified seeing the luxury goods she envisioned showing off on the Gram being ruined, right in front of her eyes.

"Yo Harper, I can't believe you doing this dumb shit!" He roared, finally losing his cool. Jamari started to storm toward her, until she raised that Glock, aiming it firmly at his chest.

"Back tha fuck up, or else," Harper threatened, nodding her head, tossing out the last bag from the trunk. But she wasn't done yet. She reached back in her purse and brandished the knife she always kept on her too. She proceeded to walk around Jamari's brand new black on black Camaro Coupe ZL1 and slashed each tire.

"You bitch! I'ma fuck you up!" Jamari uttered viciously, ready to break Harper's neck. But she wasn't worried. She was the one holding the gun.

"Ya lovebirds can walk the fuck home, hand in hand. So who's the bitch now," Harper mocked, going back to her car.

"Harper, you are fuckin' certifiable, like seriously," Taliyah kept repeating as she stared back looking at Jamari. He was having a complete meltdown, while the girl he was with, was picking up purses, shoes and clothes, trying to salvage whatever items she could.

"Jamari betta be happy I didn't bust out them windows and key his car too," she snarled. "I bet that nigga learned today not to disrespect me," Harper scoffed, driving off.

Chapter Two

LOVE HATE

You Have Been Warned

"Harper, answer the damn phone!" Her Mother screamed from the kitchen, but she ignored the request.

"I can't! I'm getting dressed, and I'm already running late!" Harper yelled back, as she stared at her reflection in the full length mirror, debating which shoes complimented her outfit best.

Harper could hear her Mother walking down the hallway towards her bedroom. She was about to get up and close her door, but got distracted when she saw Jamari's photo pop up on her iPhone.

"Aren't you gonna answer the phone?" her Mother asked in an harsh tone.

"Nope." Harper tossed her iPhone down. "I think I'll go with the strappy heels," she said grabbing her purse, and walking towards the door as if her Mother wasn't blocking the entryway.

"Harper, I'm not moving until you tell me what's going on between you and Jamari."

"I really need to go. You're going to make me later than I already am," Harper complained.

"Then I suggest you talk fast."

"I slashed his tires," Harper shrugged, choosing to leave out the part about wielding a gun.

"Why in the hell would you do that?"

"If you must know, it's because he was running around the mall, with some basic ass chick, that he took on a shopping spree. Money, he coulda spent on me." Harper fussed, becoming angry again like the incident just happened yesterday, instead of over a week ago.

"So, you out here slashing tires over shopping sprees." Harper's Mother cringed with disapproval.

"He cheated on me and disrespected me for

everybody to see," Harper snapped, making allowances for her method of retaliation.

"Oh, like you the first girl that's got cheated on." Her Mother couldn't help but shake her head. "Where did I go wrong, 'cause you ain't learned shit from me."

"Ma, I don't have time for this. Taliyah and Amina are waiting for me."

"They can keep waiting. You need to listen to what I have to say, so sit down," she ordered her daughter. Harper reluctantly sat down on her bed, and sent a text to Taliyah, while fighting the urge to curse her Mother out.

"I'm listening."

"You better be, or you're gonna end up just like me." That statement garnered Harper's attention. She put her phone down and stared up at her Mother. "You're not a teenager anymore."

"I know how old I am. Jamari threw me an elaborate party for my twenty-first birthday. You remember, you were there," Harper shot back sarcastically.

"Of course I remember, and I told you then, you needed to leave these dope boys alone. They flash a lot of cash, but that lifestyle will leave them dead or doing double digits in a federal prison, just like yo' father. But you refuse to leave these drug dealers alone."

'There's nothing wrong with liking nice things, isn't that what you always told me."

"Yeah, but I also told you to get a man with some real money... legitimate money. Don't conveniently leave that part out. You out here slashing tires over bullshit things like shopping sprees. Your father spent all his money on lawyer fees, trying to win a case that he couldn't beat, but at least he left us with this house. What do you think Jamari gon' leave you with besides a baby you can't afford to take care of."

"I ain't having no babies no time soon."

"I used to say the same thing, until I got pregnant with you. Your father promised he would always take care of us, but that was before the money dried up. Promises don't mean shit when you left alone, and have a child to feed. You know why I named you Harper?"

"Here we go again," Harper grumbled. "Yes, because Harper's Bazaar was your favorite magazine. You've told me this a million times," she sighed, rolling her eyes.

"Well I'm going to tell you a million and one more times. When I was pregnant, and I found out I was having a girl, I had your whole life planned out. I'd turn the pages of Harper's

Bazaar looking at all of the beautiful and expensive clothes, shoes, and jewelry the women were wearing. I would always say when my daughter grew up, she would be able to have everything these women in this magazine had, and so much more. And..."

"And you thought naming me Harper would speak what your heart desired into existence." She cut her Mother off, finishing her sentence. "Like I said, I've heard this story a million times. I'm trying to live up to your expectations," Harper remarked sharply, holding up her pink quilted Chanel purse.

"Fuck that bag! I did better than my Mother, and I expect you to do better than me. You ain't neva been interested in school. All you've ever wanted to do was dress and rest. So you need to listen and take my advice. Stop wasting your time and youth on these drug dealers, and find someone who can provide you with real financial security. Or you'll end up being just another pretty girl with nothing to show for, but a few trinkets."

Harper's Mother put her on notice, sounding the alarm. It was now up to her daughter to decide, if she would take heed to the warning, or continue down the path she was on, and be another example of a cautionary tale.

Chapter Three

Shiesty Season

"We doing valet or what?" Harper asked her friends when they pulled up to the new hotspot Première, a five star restaurant in Midtown Atlanta.

"Not yet, I need to fix my eyelash first," Amina said from the backseat. "Pull over in the parking lot for a minute."

"Girl, I told you to stop gluing on lashes, and get you some extensions," Taliyah smacked.

"Them shits be looking mad crazy to me. I prefer a more natural look," Amina explained.

"My shit do look natural," Taliyah scoffed, sounding insulted. "You know they come in different styles just like them fake lashes you be buying."

"I hear you," Amina said dismissively, looking in the mirror, getting her eyelash together.

"Yo look at that Lambo truck that just pulled up," Harper announced, putting an end to the eyelash debate. Taliyah and Amina both placed their attention squarely on the 2021 Arancio Borealis (orange) Lamborghini Urus with the Pearl Capsule appearance package. The 23-inch wheels, black trim pieces on the roof, rear diffuser, spoiler, and chiseled bodywork with hulking proportions, made the Italian monster a true showstopper.

"Bitch, that muthafucka so damn cold!" Taliyah shouted.

"Is the niggas we meeting, in that shit?" Harper asked excitedly.

"I fuckin' wish." Amina sucked her teeth. "They gettin' some money out here in these streets, but not them type of coins. It's probably some rapper or NBA player," she reasoned.

"The driver gettin' out the car now!" Taliyah nudged Harper on the shoulder, unable to contain her enthusiasm. The three friends remained fixated on the vehicle, anxious to see who the owner of that prized showpiece was.

"That nigga wearing a suit. He look clean, but I ain't gettin' rapper or athlete vibes. He seem older too," Harper commented.

"Wait, hold on a minute," Amina rolled down the window. "I know that dude."

"You know him? How you know that muthafucka?" Taliyah questioned with skepticism.

"I don't know him...I meant to say I know of him. That's Mahoney Monroe. We were discussing him in my microeconomics class last week," Amina clarified.

"Who!?" Taliyah gave a puzzled look. "I ain't never heard of him."

"Mahoney Monroe... he sound like he got two last names," Harper cracked.

"Let me enlighten you ladies." Amina switched on her college girl professional voice. "Mahoney Monroe is the principal founder, chairman and chief executive of Prospect Equity Partners, a private equity and venture capital firm. The private equity firm, buys and sells enterprise software companies."

"Fuck all that, what's his money looking like?" Harper wanted to know.

"He's a billionaire." Amina declared.

"Excuse me...like with a b not a m?" Taliyah questioned, completely stunned.

"Yep. That's what I said, a billionaire bitches," Amina winked.

"I got my billions up, fuckin' with dem white folks, now I don't give a fuck, cause I'm richer than dem white folks. Lamborghini trucks..." Harper rapped. "You know I had to drop my favorite line from that Let's Do It Remix. It was only fitting," she laughed.

"Harper, you a fool!" Amina chuckled.

"I would be a fool if I didn't try to dig these nails into that Mahoney billionaire dude."

"Sorry, you'll have to find your own billionaire. He's a very married man." Amina informed them.

"That must be his wife he just opened the passenger door for," Taliyah said, as the attractive tall woman stepped out the truck.

"Come on ya, the guys we're meeting are already sitting down in the restaurant waiting for us," Amina told them reading the text message. She put on a little more lipstick before getting out the car. Harper was so preoccupied watching Mahoney and his wife's every move, that she didn't even notice her friends had gotten out the car.

"Girl, what are you doing... come on, I'm hungry!" Taliyah called out, snapping Harper out of her daze.

Harper glanced at her reflection in the rear-view mirror and quickly dabbed on some clear lip gloss. She fluffed out her curly hair and headed inside the restaurant. While her friends were searching for the table where their dates were sitting, Harper was doing her own surveillance, but for someone else.

"I'll meet you all at the table. I have to use the restroom right quick," Harper said, hastily walking away before her friends could stop her.

Harper!" Taliyah called out, but her friend had already disappeared. Once Harper spotted her target, she was on a mission. She knew more than likely, this would be her only opportunity to make a move, and had to strike now.

Harper observed Mahoney leave his wife at the table and walk towards the restroom. She immediately headed in his direction. With limited time to orchestrate a plan, she went with the easiest way to get his attention. She stayed slightly back, keeping her distance, waiting for the precise moment to act. There was no wiggle room for missteps, it had to be done without error.

With no new sighting of Mahoney, Harper became flustered. After the third man came out of the restroom and none of them were him, she started to conclude she must've missed him. She was ready to give up and walk away, until a few seconds later he emerged. *Oh fuck!* Harper shouted to herself, but without hesitation she made her move.

"Would you stop yelling at me! I'm out with some friends. I'm leaving shortly," Harper fussed, pretending to be in the midst of an intense phone conversation. Right as Mahoney was about to cross her path, she dropped her purse and everything spilled out. The objects landed at the tip of his Derby brown patina calfskin shoes, with Goodyear welt construction from the Dior Homme Francois Premier collection.

"I have to call you back!" She yelled into the phone, keeping the farce going. "I'm so, so sorry. I feel utterly stupid. I wasn't paying attention."

Harper sounded very convincing. She made sure not to make eye contact with Mahoney just yet. Instead she introduced him to her perky breasts first. They were on full display in a lace white bra, due to her lowcut blouse.

"No need to apologize, accidents happen," Mahoney said, helping her pick up the items. Right on cue, Harper glanced up at him, as both were kneeling down on the floor and they locked eyes. She knew at that very moment, she had him. "Is this the perfume you're wearing?"

"Yes, it's my favorite," Harper smiled. Casually placing her hand on top of his when she took the bottle of Love In Black by Creed from him.

"I understand why." Mahoney leaned in closer to her. Harper let her hair brush against his face, and then her breasts, before pulling back.

"Again, I'm so sorry, but thank you for being such a gentleman." Harper beamed sweetly. "You should let me treat you to lunch. Just to show my appreciation." Mahoney hesitated for a moment. "I apologize, I hope I didn't make you uncomfortable."

"No, don't apologize. I would like for us to have lunch. What's your name?"

"Harper."

"Harper, I'm Mahoney. It's nice to meet you. Here, put your number in my phone."

"Nice to meet you too. I'm looking forward to our lunch, so don't take too long to call me."

"I won't," Mahoney said, bending down to pick up a tube of lip gloss. "Almost missed this." He handed it to Harper, gripping her fingers. Once again their eyes locked. They both seemed to be stopping themselves from leaning forward and engaging in a passionate kiss.

"I really need to use the bathroom." Harper purposely broke their gaze, turning away, intent on leaving Mahoney wanting more.

Harper waited until she was safe in one of the restroom stalls before letting a huge grin spread across her face. "Yes!" She pumped her fist in the air. "I'm going to make you proud Ma." She continued smiling as she walked to her table. Although that smile faded, when Harper realized Mahoney and his wife were both gone.

Chapter Four

Something Special

"Why the fuck you keep calling me Jamari!" Harper screamed into the phone.

"Baby, don't hang up. I just wanna talk to you, please..." he pleaded.

After Harper whipped out a gun on Jamari, and slashed his tires, he spent the first couple weeks threatening her life. But not one to be intimidated, Harper showed no fear. She kept poppin' shit, and now for the last week, Jamari had been begging her to take him back. This was typical of their dysfunctional relationship.

"Jamari, I'm over you and this bullshit that comes with dealing with yo' stupid ass."

"But I love you. I'ma do better," he promised.

"You took another chick shopping at the mall. My friends saw you. You embarrassed me."

"I know, I fucked up. I shouldn't of done that shit. But I got mad cause I heard, you was out wit' another nigga at the movies the night before."

"What tha fuck ever. I wasn't wit' no other nigga," she lied and said. But that's what they would do; fight, lie and cheat on each other, then make up. This time would've been no different, but things were about to quickly change. "Hold on for a second," Harper sulked, when another call came through. "Hello."

"Is this Harper?"

"Yes, who is this?"

"Mahoney, how are you?"

Harper perked up and started kicking her legs in the air, she was so damn happy to hear from him. "Better now. I thought you forgot about me." Giving him her tried and true combo of innocent, yet temptress voice.

"No, I had to go out of town. Are you free for lunch?"

"Sure...when?"

"In an hour."

That caught Harper completely off guard. She figured Mahoney would say tomorrow, or later in the week, but she had no intentions of keeping a billionaire waiting.

"That works."

"I have a meeting I need to attend. It should be brief, so can you meet me?"

"Of course. I'll be there."

"I'll text you the address. See you soon."

Harper was so excited, she forgot Jamari was waiting on the other line. "I have to call you back."

"Call me back!" He barked. "I been waitin' and all you got is you have to call me back."

"It's my Mother. Something happened and she needs me to pick her up. I'll call you back." Harper hung up on Jamari and rushed to take a shower and get dressed.

Harper arrived at the Waldorf Astoria in Buckhead, wearing a fitted ivory colored mini blazer dress, with double breasted buttons. She accessorized it with open toe nude pumps and a matching purse. She wanted to keep her look classy based sexy. Nothing over the top. She headed towards The Bar, which was located on the ground floor, just off the hotel lobby. When she reached the garden, it was an ideal place for a true outdoor open air, romantic lunch experience.

"Hi, I'm meeting someone here for lunch," she told the hostess.

"Your name?"

"Harper."

"Yes." The hostess gave a wide, toothy smile. "Mr. Monroe is waiting for you, follow me. She led Harper to a private terrace that overlooked the garden. "Your guest has arrived, Mr. Monroe. Please let me know if you need anything."

"Thank you, Amanda," he politely stated, then walked over and pulled out the chair for Harper. "You're even more beautiful then I remember."

"And you're even more handsome," Harper replied, and she meant it. Mahoney had the face of Larenz Tate, the height of Idris Elba, with this slight hint of nerdiness that she found absolutely adorable. He was completely different than the standard hood rich niggas she was drawn to. However, that wouldn't deter Harper from executing her typical tricks on Mahoney, but with slight modifications.

"Well thank you. I took it upon myself to order our lunch, I hope you don't mind."

"No, I don't. One less thing I have to think about. Instead of scrolling through a menu, I can look at you, as you're much more appealing."

"Good point," Mahoney chuckled.

"I didn't say that to make you laugh. What do you find so funny?"

"I'm not laughing at what you said. I guess I'm laughing at how you're making me feel."

"How is that?"

"Kinda like an awkward teenage boy."

"I must be doing something wrong, because that's definitely not how I want to make you feel."

"You're actually doing everything right. I have a condo in this hotel. After lunch, will you join me upstairs for a drink?"

"How about we go upstairs now, and have our lunch brought up after we have drinks," Harper suggested, wasting no time.

"Didn't I just say you're doing everything right."

"Then allow me to keep it up, because I don't want to disappoint you."

Harper stayed true to her word, and did not disappoint. The moment Mahoney opened the door to his dual-level penthouse, perched atop the Waldorf Astoria Buckhead Residences, she became the aggressor, and he didn't object. He enjoyed letting the young beauty take control. Especially since his powerful position in business, had him under high levels of pressure around the clock. This sexual exchange was becoming the stress reliever Mahoney needed. Harper was tearing off his custom made button down dress shirt, while simultaneously removing his belt and unfastening his pants. As she began kissing his chest, she was pleasantly surprised at how defined his pectoral muscles, better known as "pecs" were. His back was pinned to the wall, and Harper glided her hand down the center of his stomach, as she left a warm trail of kisses all the way down to his belly button.

"Do you want me to stop?" she asked in a teasing, seductive voice. Harper was on bended knee, staring up at Mahoney with lust in her eyes.

"No," was all he was able to say, before letting out a deep moan, after Harper placed his dick inside her wet mouth. There was nothing more empowering and intoxicating to Harper than having control over a penis, and by effect, the man attached to it, especially when that man was a self-made billionaire.

The visual element of watching every inch of his hard dick slip in and out of Harper's warm mouth, had Mahoney spellbound. The ease and precision her lips and tongue played with his tool, was like an irreplaceable work of art. Harper would purposely take breaks to switch her gaze from his dick, to then locking eyes with her prey.

"I love how your dick feels in my mouth." Harper told Mahoney, then went back to deep throat mode, before shifting some of the work to her hands. She wrapped her dominant hand around the shaft of his dick. Her mouth provided the warmth and wetness, and her hand provided the tightness. It almost replicated the same sensation of being inside a vagina, but the man didn't have to put in any of the work. Instead he was able to relax, be pleasured and enjoy what was happening right in front of him.

The fact that Harper appeared to be enjoying giving Mahoney head, aroused him even more. She began moving her hand plus lips in seamless sync, up and down his dick. She used her other hand to cup and gently squeeze his balls, making sure to keep her lips in the perfect head giving pout, slightly curled and pillowy. She could feel Mahoney's dick throbbing.

"Do you want to cum in my mouth?" Harper was staring up at Mahoney who was breathing heavy. He didn't answer her. Instead he gripped the back of her hair and pulled her close, pressing her lips against his. His dick was so hard he thought a blood vessel was about to explode. He couldn't even wait to take her to the bedroom. He laid Harper down on the wide plank 7" white oak floors. Mahoney pulled at her mesh G string, anticipating how good his dick would feel inside her, but first he wanted to taste her sweetness.

Harper's body released a subtle jolt at the touch of Mahoney's lips kissing her clit. His tongue swayed from side to side, as if searching for the exact spot that would take her to the brink and push her over the edge. When Harper was right at the cusp, Mahoney ripped open her blazer dress, so his tongue could lead a warm trail up to the center of her stomach, all the way back up to her mouth. As if in unison, the moment his tongue entered her mouth, his dick slid between her legs. Harper relaxed her body once she believed his thick tool was all the way in, but then he pushed the remaining inches inside of her, causing her to flinch from the discomfort. She grabbed onto Mahoney's back, biting down on his shoulder from the pain that quickly turned into what felt like eternal euphoria.

Chapter Five

Confessions

Harper opened her eyes surrounded by city and mountain views. For a moment she thought she was dreaming and sleeping on a cloud. But in reality she was lying in a massive bed, enshrouded by the plushest duvet cover she'd ever seen or felt in her life. Once Harper remembered where she was, she sat up in the bed, and noticed Mahoney was standing near the outdoor fireplace, talking on the phone. She could see him clearly, because there was a continuous transition from inside the bedroom to outside, with the

NanaWall glass accordion doors opening to the expansive patio.

"You're awake," Mahoney said, stepping back inside the bedroom.

"I woke up, and honestly for a second, I had no idea where I was. How long have I been asleep?"

"For a few hours."

"I feel so embarrassed," Harper blushed, grabbing a pillow to cover her face. "Why didn't you wake me up?"

"I liked watching you sleep, and you have nothing to be embarrassed about. We both put in a lot of work," Mahoney cracked. "You should be tired."

"Then why aren't you tired?" she questioned.

"I was, but I had to get up. There was an oversea call I needed to make."

"I see. Well, let me get up and get dressed," Harper said, removing the duvet cover from her naked body. "I'm sure you have a lot to do, so I better get going."

"You don't have to go."

"That's sweet of you to be so polite, but you're clearly a very busy man, and I don't want to inconvenience you."

"You're not an inconvenience, and what

I should have said was, I don't want you to go. Please stay."

"Really?" Harper smiled.

"Yes, really." Mahoney walked over to the bed and kissed her on the forehead. "Are you hungry?"

"Hungry isn't a strong enough word. I'm starving!" She exclaimed.

"Good. I already ordered us dinner."

"Speaking of dinner, that night I met you at the restaurant, when I came out the bathroom I was looking for you, but you were gone. I started thinking you were ghosting me."

"Nothing like that. I have a confession to make." Mahoney's tone turned serious.

"Confession...sounds so intense." Harper giggled nervously. She was doing her best to give the façade of a seductress, but a sweet-natured naïve one.

"There's something I do need to tell you."

"What is it?" she asked in her most ingenuous voice. But Harper was confident she knew exactly what his confession would be.

"I'm married. The night I met you, I was at the restaurant with my wife. I left, because I didn't want you to get the wrong impression of me."

"Wow." She pretended that Mahoney's admission had rendered her speechless.

"I know I should've been upfront with you."

"I guess it's a good thing I'm not married too," she joked, switching things up. Harper wanted to make it difficult for Mahoney to get an accurate read on her state of mind.

"You're taking this better than I thought you would."

"Am I disappointed, of course, but I guess I shouldn't be surprised. You're a handsome man, who is obviously extremely successful," Harper noted, glancing around his over 7,000 sqft. penthouse, as if she was clueless to the fact, that she already knew he was married and a billionaire. "So of course you would have a wife by your side. But I do think it's best that I go."

"Please don't." Mahoney grabbed Harper's arm to stop her from walking away.

"I don't think this is where I need to be."

"Don't say that. I made a mistake. I should've been honest with you. I'm sorry."

"I really have to go. I don't want to be here." Harper protested one last time, although she had no intentions of going anywhere. But she knew it was important to make it appear, her feelings were genuinely hurt.

"Please don't go." Mahoney continued to hold on to her arm. Refusing to release Harper from his grasp. "At least stay for dinner."

That dinner turned into dessert, a bottle of wine, and another amazing sex session. The two of them shared undeniable chemistry. It seemed to be the most important prerequisite Mahoney required, to make him decide to keep Harper as a permanent fixture in his life—at least for the time being.

"You ruined my dress," Harper laughed, when she got out of bed, after they finished having sex again. She grabbed the dress off the chair and held it up. "I can't even button it. You tore them all off."

"What can I say... I'm not a very patient man. I just had to have you."

"Cute. I guess I should be flattered, but that isn't going to solve my problem. Am I supposed to get on the elevator in my bra and panties."

"I wouldn't have an issue with that, however I'm pretty sure it's against hotel policy," Mahoney smiled. "I guess that means you're stuck here and can't leave," he surmised.

"Are you saying you want me to stay?"

"I didn't ask you to go, did I."

"But what about your wife? I'm pretty sure

she would have a problem with me being here."

"I'm pretty sure you're right, but you don't have to worry about that. My wife doesn't have a key to this place. So does that mean you'll stay?"

"How could I ever say no to you. But I still need to go home and get some clothes."

"I'll leave you one of my credit cards. Tomorrow you can call downstairs to the concierge, and they'll have a personal shopper get you whatever you want. Does that work for you?"

"Yeah, it does."

"Good. I like when I can come up with a solution to a problem." Mahoney nodded his head, pleased with himself. "Now come get back in this bed with me."

Harper didn't hesitate to indulge his request. After plenty of practice, she believed she was finally putting her sexual skills to optimal use. As far as Harper was concerned, Mahoney was the ultimate catch, even if he was a married man.

Chapter Six

LOVE HATE

Strategic Moves

"Bitch, whose dick is you sucking?!" Was the welcoming Harper received from Taliyah, when she and Amina met her at the hotel bar inside the Waldorf Astoria.

"Yo' ass still a fool! I'm so happy to see you. I missed my besties!" Harper ran over to Taliyah and Amina, giving them both a huge hug.

"We missed you too!" Both ladies said in unison, as they all sat down in a booth.

"How have you been? We ain't seen you in weeks. Your Mother said, you've barely been home. And how the fuck you staying up in the Waldorf Astoria?"

"Damn, Taliyah. Can you slow down and give her a chance to answer your question." Amina balked. "She can only answer one at a time."

"Sorry. Ya know how I get when I'm anxious."

"So, where do I start," Harper said carefreely, taking a sip of champagne.

"We can start at my initial question, whose dick are you sucking?" Taliyah cracked, pouring herself some champagne too.

"If you must know, Mahoney Monroe."

Harper's staggering announcement left her friends dumbfounded. There was this lingering silence. Taliyah and Amina stared at each other, then directed their eyes back at Harper, who was busy pouring her second glass of champagne.

"Okay, you can stop playing Harper." Amina rolled her eyes.

"What she said!" Taliyah chimed in agreeing with Amina. "Now who is the new man occupying all your time?"

"I just told you. Have I ever lied on some dick before...come on now." Harper flung her arm up like, bitches please.

"Are you fuckin' serious?" Amina's voice went low. She leaned in closely, as if she was privy to some top secret intel, and such material would cause exceptionally grave damage to national security if made public.

"Girl, why are you whispering, and please move back. There's no need for you to be all up in my face like that," Harper frowned.

"Fuck!!" Taliyah banged her hand down on the table. "You are serious. I am so jealous right now. How in the fuck did you pull this off," Taliyah was dying to know and so was Amina.

"Do explain. It's not like you and Mahoney run in the same circles. How did you meet him?" Amina threw her question in there too.

"I actually met him that night we saw him at the restaurant."

"The night we saw him with his wife? That was like two months ago." Amina was beside herself. She couldn't stop fidgeting in her chair.

"You've been getting billionaire caliber dick for all these weeks, and kept that shit to yourself. Let me bow down to you bitch, because I would've let that slip in less than twenty-four hours," Taliyah admitted.

"When there's a lot of money on the line, you have to be more strategic with how you move," Harper smirked.

"I can't lie, I'm shocked and impressed. So

he's been paying for you to stay in this hotel?" Amina needed answers.

"He owns a condo in here," Harper divulged.

"Really? I thought the Waldorf Astoria was just an expensive ass hotel. Never knew there were condos too," Taliyah said.

"Shit me neither. His spot is a penthouse though. It has like an elliptical staircase, 360-degree views from every room, heated floors, a bunch of exotic stones in all the bathrooms, kitchen and shit, just freakin' amazing. I had no idea people was living like that. It literally blew my mind."

"So wait, he has you staying in his penthouse...what about his wife?" Amina was digging for all the details.

"Clearly he's a serial cheater." Harper had determined. "Because he told me, his wife doesn't have a key to his place here. Which means it's his fuck pad." She stated matter of factly. "But that's irrelevant to me. I'm just trying to secure a permanent position on his team. Hell, I don't mind if I'm just part of the rotation, as long as he keeps spoiling me. "

"Has he taken you shopping yet?" Taliyah's eyes widened, completely enthralled with Harper's new life.

"Shopping…he ain't no low budget nigga like Jamari. He left me a credit card with my own personal shopper. You should see all the shit I have upstairs," Harper bragged.

"OMG!! Take me upstairs. I wanna see. Please," Taliyah begged.

"Not yet. I haven't secured my position."

"What you mean, he got you living good! Seems like shit is secure to me," Taliyah popped.

"He's a billionaire. I'm not saying he just runnin' around here wasting money on bitches, but this ain't hurtin' his pockets. I've been playing my position just right so far."

"And how is that?" Amina inquired.

"Always happy to see him, but not clingy. Always look sexy, but I never try to seduce him. I wait for him to ask for it, and then I fuck and suck him just right. Always available, but never around until he wants me to be. Always sweet, but never annoying. I keep this up just a little bit longer, Mahoney Monroe won't be able to imagine his life without me in it," Harper winked confidently.

"Girl, you need to teach a class. Shit, I don't even need a billionaire. I ain't greedy. I'll be perfectly content with a high six figure nigga." Taliyah stated eagerly, ready for her own come up.

"We'll discuss that next time you all stop by for lunch, because I have to go."

"You have to go already?" Amina sounded disappointed to see her friend leaving so soon.

"Yep. Remember what I said, always available but never around until he wants me to be. He just sent me a text, duty calls, dolls. But order whatever you want. They already know the bill is on me. Love you ladies!" Harper beamed, blowing kisses. "See you soon." She waved goodbye and headed upstairs. Harper did not like to keep Mahoney waiting.

Chapter Seven

LOVE HATE

Where Is The Love

"I think I might be addicted to you," Mahoney said, kissing Harper's nipple while they laid in bed. They'd just finished having sex for the third time, and he already missed being inside her.

"I hope so, because I've been addicted to you since the first time we made love. Nobody has ever made me feel the way that you do." Harper gazed at Mahoney with an angelic spark in her eyes, gently stroking his chiseled jawline. She had finally mastered how to make him feel like the most important man in the world.

"I was thinking we could get away this weekend. We can go anywhere you want. I'm sure you're tired of us being confined to this condo. Where would you like to go?" Mahoney wanted to know.

"Baby, you don't have to take me on a trip. I love being right here with you. I cross my heart."

"You have this way of saying exactly what I need to hear. I love that about you," Mahoney smiled, kissing Harper on the lips. "I still want us to get away from here. Show you off. Let everyone see how lucky I am to have such a gorgeous girlfriend," he boasted.

"Seriously...now I'm getting excited. Spending the entire weekend with you. Waking up in your arms. That sounds amazing," Harper gushed.

"It will be. So where do you want to go?"

"Surprise me!" Harper clapped her hands enthusiastically.

"I like that idea. We can leave tomorrow after I wrap up my last meeting."

"So soon? You don't even know where we're going or what flights are available."

"I have a private jet, no preparation needed."

"I have never been on a private jet in my life! This really is exciting!"

"I must admit, I'm looking forward to spending the weekend with you too. It will be the perfect romantic getaway," Mahoney promised, getting out the bed. "I'm sorry, but I have to go," he said putting his clothes back on.

"You don't have to apologize to me for going home to your wife. You've been doing that a lot lately. It was my decision to keep seeing you after you told me you were married."

"I know but..." Mahoney paused for a moment.

"But what?"

"I'm not sure if it's because you're always so understanding, but lately for some reason, I feel guilty when I leave you here alone. You're so young, beautiful, and such a loving person. You deserve to have me here with you. I promise to make it up to you this weekend." Mahoney gave Harper one last kiss goodbye and walked out the door.

"You're finally home." Lana greeted her husband with a dry smile, when he came in the bedroom and headed straight to the master bath.

"Yeah, I had a busy day. My last meeting ran

late," Mahoney called out, turning on the shower.

"That's been happening a lot lately." Lana got out the bed and headed into the bathroom to interrogate her husband. "Who was the meeting with?"

"I had a meeting with a private equity company that does a lot of business in South Africa. I'm considering doing a little more expanding." Mahoney wasn't making any eye contact with his wife, hoping it would stop her from asking him any additional questions.

"I'm sure you'll make it happen if you choose to. You always find a way to get what you want." Lana's statement came across as having nothing to do with business, and was much more personal.

"Can you hand me a face cloth, I forgot to get one before getting in the shower."

"I'm picking my parents up from the airport in the morning," Lana said, handing her husband the washcloth. "I tried to get them to stay at a hotel, but they insisted on spending the weekend here with us."

"I thought your parents were coming next weekend?"

"The dinner party is Saturday. Please don't tell me you forgot it's my birthday on Saturday."

"Of course I didn't forget Lana," Mahoney lied. "I just didn't realize they were coming tomorrow."

"Why would they come next weekend when my birthday is Saturday?" Lana's question lingered in the air, but she wasn't letting shit slide. She pressed on. "Answer the question, Mahoney. It doesn't make sense for my parents to come next weekend, if we're having my dinner party Saturday. They always come for my birthday every year."

"You're right. I have a lot on my mind. Like I said, I had a busy day."

"Too busy to remember it's my birthday on Saturday?"

"Lana, I'm exhausted. I had an extremely long day at work. I'm not up for arguing with you tonight."

"You never seem up to doing anything with me lately," Lana sniped, but Mahoney ignored his wife. He knew exactly what she was alluding to.

Although Lana was a very attractive woman, she didn't exude that sultriness her husband had become drawn to, which meant Mahoney barely had sex with his wife anymore. The lack of intimacy had left an empty hole in her soul. She felt the only thing that could fill that hole was a child.

After years of trying to conceive, Lana went to see a fertility specialist and found out due to some inner tissue scarring, she had blocked fallopian tubes. She so desperately wanted to have a baby, she went through an invasive procedure to open the tube. The surgery seemed to be a success when a few months later, Lana found out she was pregnant. Unfortunately, it turned out to be an ectopic pregnancy. Her physician soon determined, due to the health of her tubes, Lana would never be able to conceive again.

She had spent the last couple of years, trying to convince her husband that they should have a baby using a surrogate, or even consider adoption, but he showed no interest. There was no denying the emotional distance between them, was taking a toll on their marriage. But Mahoney was the love of her life. Make no mistake, Lana was never going to let her husband go.

Chapter Eight

Before The Storm

Harper had spent all day getting prepared for her weekend getaway. She got her hair and nails done, did some shopping at Phipps Plaza, focusing primarily on some sexy lingerie to wear during their retreat. Although Harper began plotting from the second she laid eyes on Mahoney Monroe, and found out who he was, she never imagined their affair would feel this magical. They had been seeing each other for three months now, and instead of slowing down, it was only heating up.

"Well look who the wind blew in!" Harper's Mother exclaimed when her daughter came prancing through the front door.

"I'm sorry I haven't stopped by to visit sooner, but things have been a little crazy for me."

"Yeah I bet. Taliyah came by here the other day to pick up a dress and some shoes you said she could borrow. She told me all about that new man you're seeing."

"He's pretty amazing."

"I heard he was a lot older than you too."

"True. That just means he knows how to treat a woman."

"Um-hum. It also means that he's probably married."

"We're actually going away for the weekend, so I can't stay long," Harper said, choosing not to respond to her Mother's comment. "I got a few things for you when I was at the mall today, and wanted to drop them off before I went out of town." Harper handed the bags filled with the overly priced items to her Mother.

"Thanks." Her Mother seemed unimpressed. "Harper, you better be careful," she cautioned. "If this man is as amazing as you claim, his wife will never give him up. People are capable of doing all sorts of crazy things, in the name of love."

"You told me I needed to leave these drug dealers alone and level up. Well, I leveled up to the highest you can go, with this man. So instead of criticizing, congratulate me."

"I want you to win, Harper. But just know, this game you're playing, you can come out the loser, so prepare accordingly."

"Thanks for the advice. I have to go." Harper stormed out her Mother's house pissed off. She had been in a state of euphoria all day, and her high was ruined in a matter of minutes. She was determined to shake off the fucked up mood her Mother left her in, and knew exactly what to do, to make that happen. Harper put on that Cardi B, and let it blast through her Meridian surround sound system.

Look, once upon a time, man, I heard that I was ugly
Came from a bitch who nigga wanna fuck on me
I said my face bomb, ass tight
Racks stack up Shaq height
Jewelry on me, flashlight
I been lit since last night
Hit him with that good, good
Make a nigga act right

Broke boys don't deserve no pussy
(I know that's right!)

Harper was having her own mini concert in the car, as she was rapping along with Cardi B. She was so enthralled in the music, she didn't realize Mahoney had sent her a text, until she was pulling up to the valet at the Waldorf Astoria. Once again her high came crashing down.

Baby I'm sorry. I can't get away. I promise to make it up to you.

Harper was ready to demolish the entire lobby of the Waldorf Astoria, as she made her way to the penthouse. *How dare that muthafucka stand me up. I'ma fuckin' curse his ass out!* Harper was screaming in her head, while the elevator was going up to the top floor.

"Harper take a deep breath and calm down." She spoke those words out loud, the moment she was alone behind closed doors. She read Mahoney's text message once again, then tossed her phone across the bed. Harper was dealing with the downside of being the other woman, and it was fucking her head up. She didn't leave the penthouse the entire weekend, and refused to speak with anyone, although the one person she did want to talk to, never called.

"Good morning, beautiful."

Harper opened her eyes, and Mahoney was sitting on the bed next to her with a huge bouquet of flowers.

"Good morning." She sat up in bed and took in the scent of the gorgeous floral arrangement.

"How was your weekend?"

"If you'd called, or had come to see me, you would already know the answer to that," Harper scoffed, throwing the flowers on the floor, as she was getting out of bed.

"Baby, I'm so sorry. I completely forgot it was my wife's birthday. We had a dinner party, and her family was staying at the house the entire weekend." Mahoney thought his explanation would soften the mood, but instead, it sent Harper into a fit of rage.

"You think I give a fuck about your wife's birthday! Fuck you and your wife!" The sound of her voice thundered through the room.

Mahoney was completely taken aback. Harper had never raised her voice in his presence, let alone cursed at him. If anything, he would've described her as soft spoken. "I need you to calm down."

"Calm down...you want me to calm?! It was you who came up with the idea of going out of town for the weekend. You promised me the perfect romantic getaway, and then you send me some bullshit text, saying you can't come. You're a fuckin' piece of shit!" Harper roared.

If Mahoney wasn't witnessing this rampage Harper was on with his own eyes, he would've never believed she was even capable of this sort of wrath. And she was not done yet.

"I went and got this stuff for our trip," Harper fumed, hurling all the lingerie she purchased in Mahoney's face. "And all you have for me is a weak ass sorry, and some fuckin' flowers. You can shove those flowers up your ass! I will never let you hurt me again. NEVER!!"

Shock left Mahoney paralyzed. He was firmly positioned on the bed. It wasn't until Harper started throwing on some clothes, and he realized she was leaving, did he make a move.

"Where are you going?" he stood up suddenly.

"Away from you. I'm done!"

"Okay, this is getting out of hand. Let's sit down and discuss what's going on with you." Mahoney wanted to have a calm discussion, but this had escalated to a storm.

"I'm not one of your fuckin' business clients, that you can try to reason with. We have nothing to discuss!" Harper pushed him with such force, when she brushed past him, grabbing her purse and car keys.

Mahoney was a wealthy and powerful businessman, who was used to being in control, and maintaining his composure. But watching the woman he had become emotionally entwined with, about to walk out his life, sent him into panic mode.

Harper was almost at the end of the hallway, when Mahoney came chasing after her. "I can't let you leave me." He flung Harper around, pinning her body against the wall.

"Get off me!" She yelled, as Mahoney towered over her. "I hate you!" Harper screamed over and over again, landing punches on him wherever she could. The spike in her adrenaline temporarily increased her strength. But at this point, both were highly stressed, which triggered a combative fight-or-flight dynamic between the lovers. Mahoney was fighting for Harper to stay, but she was determined to get away.

"I can't let you go!" Mahoney had locked his hand over Harper's mouth. It was easy for him to overpower the petite beauty. But the harder Harper fought back, the more eager they became to unleash their pent up sexual energy on each other. Although Harper was doing her best, not to give into her desires, Mahoney was resolute in his quest to break her down. He flung Harper over his shoulder, while she continued to protest.

"I'm done with you. Now put me down!" Harper demanded.

"You will never be done with me!" Mahoney threw Harper on the bed, and began to roughly peel off her clothes.

"I hate you!" She cried, swinging wildly. But those cries of anger soon turned to moans of pleasure when Mahoney thrusted himself inside her. The intense energy translated into erotic desire, and had his dick rock hard.

"Damn this pussy so wet." Mahoney was breathing heavily. His strokes became more forceful, wanting to fully penetrate and submerge as deep as he could go. Their passion and intensity had Harper's entire body shivering with arousal and pleasure. Once they reached their climax, the menacing storm dissipated, and them surviving it, brought them even closer.

"I love you." Mahoney whispered those three words to Harper for the very first time.

"I love you too." She closed her eyes, and the two lovers fell into a deep sleep, wrapped in each other's arms.

Chapter Nine

LOVE HATE

After The Love Is Gone

"After all these months, I can't believe you and Mr. Money Bags are still going strong," Taliyah said, leaning back on the plush living room sofa, enjoying her strawberry Bellini.

"We went through a rough period a few weeks back, but I'm hoping things will work out between us."

"You better do more than hope. Look how this man got you living. And that fuckin' kitchen." Taliyah shook her head, thinking about the antiqued mirror backsplash found prominently displayed above the cooktop, which was wrapped in natural stone countertops. "You know how much I enjoy cooking. If I had a kitchen that looked like that, I'd probably sleep in there."

"No doubt. Mahoney has me living extremely well." Harper's head was down, and she was cradling her wine glass.

"You have everything any woman would want, but you're sitting over there looking mad sad, like you lost your best friend. But I'm right here. I know when something is wrong. Talk to me."

"You want the truth." Harper glanced up with regret and somberness in her eyes.

"Always. What's the point of having a best friend if you can't tell them the truth."

"I've fallen in love with Mahoney. A man who will never be mine," Harper professed.

"Say it ain't so. We've known each other since the second grade. I ain't never heard you say you're in love with any man. Are you sure?"

"Positive. A few weeks ago we were supposed to go out of town together for the weekend."

"I remember that. You were so excited. I thought ya went. You didn't go?"

Harper shook her head no. "I was too angry to tell anybody, because I didn't want to talk about it. He completely broke my heart that day." Without warning, Harper started bawling. This pent up pain she'd been suppressing came flooding out.

Taliyah ran over to Harper, and held her tightly. She had never seen her friend this vulnerable before. She wasn't sure what to do to make her feel better, so Taliyah just continued to hold her until she was all cried out. But Harper quickly tried to pull herself together, when she realized Mahoney was calling her.

"Hey babe." She answered sweetly," wiping away her tears. Harper was doing her best to hide the fact, that only a few seconds ago, she was crying her heart out on her best friend's shoulder.

"Are you okay? You sound like something is wrong."

"I'm fine. I was laying down, falling asleep. Then I saw you calling. I'm just a little out of it. How are you?"

"I'll be better when I see you tonight."

"You're coming over?" Harper's mood instantly brightened up.

"Yes. I miss you, and I want to be with you tonight. I wish I could be with you every night."

"I wish that too. It's not the same when you're not here with me."

"I don't want to be without you either. Just know, I'm figuring out a way where I can be there with you all the time."

"You mean that?" Harper didn't want to get her hopes up, only to have her heart shattered again.

"Yes, I promise. And Harper, I will not break my promise to you ever again. But please be patient with me. I am trying to make it right with you. You have to believe me."

"I do baby and I'll be patient."

"Thank you. I'll see you later on tonight."

"Okay."

"And Harper, I love you."

"I love you too, Mahoney."

When Mahoney got home, his intention was to take a shower, get dressed, and leave right back out to go see Harper. But that changed when he entered the bedroom he shared with his wife.

"Lana, what are you doing here, and why are you standing there in the dark?" he was alarmed when he turned on the light, and found his wife staring out at the terrace, while holding their wedding picture.

"Don't I have a right to be here...this is our home...our bedroom."

"You know what I meant. I thought you had a social event tonight for one of those nonprofits you raise money for," Mahoney said dismissively, starting to undress as he headed to the bathroom to take a shower.

"No, I don't have an event tonight, but we need to talk."

"Not right now. I have to get ready, I'm running late for a business meeting."

"What sort of business meeting are you having this time of night?"

"Some associates just came in town, and I'm taking them out for dinner."

"Since I'm already dressed, I can go with you."

Mahoney stopped at the entryway of his walk in closet, and turned to face his wife. "That won't be necessary. No one is bringing their significant other."

"I'm not your significant other, I'm your wife!" Lana shouted.

"What is wrong with you...why are you yelling?"

"What is wrong with me... the question should be what the hell is wrong with you!" Lana's voice was trembling. "We've been married for over ten years. First you forgot my birthday, and now you don't even remember that today is our wedding anniversary." You could hear every ounce of her pain when she spoke.

"I apologize."

"That's all you got?" Lana wasn't sure if she was more offended about his nonchalant apology, or angry that her husband sincerely forgot, that today was their wedding anniversary.

"I don't know what else to say." Mahoney chose to minimize the hurt he caused his wife. "We can discuss it further tomorrow."

"That hussy you're running around with, has you so open, that you're not even going to pretend you give a damn about our marriage!"

"I don't know what you're talking about."

"I know about your affair with that twenty-one year old twit. What's her name again... Harper."

"Why ask me, you seem to have all the answers." His flippant response, made his wife feel he was taunting her.

Lana raised her hand so far back, that when it landed on the right side of Mahoney's face, she slapped the spit out his mouth.

"Do you feel better now?" his tone was condescending. "I let you slap me once, but it won't happen again."

"Fuck you, Mahoney!" Lana lunged at her husband, this time with her fists balled. He blocked her swings and held her wrists tightly.

"Don't put your hands on me!" He barked, pushing her down on the bed.

"I've dealt with you fuckin' around for years, because you never threw it in my face. But I'll be damned, if I'm going to let you run around town with that lowdown hoe, blatantly disrespecting me!" Lana screamed.

"You have options. You can always file for divorce. I'll give you a generous settlement. Much more than what you're guaranteed in our post-nuptial agreement."

Lana slumped over like she'd been punched in the stomach. Mahoney hadn't beat her with his fists, but his words had a more powerful impact. Within a matter of seconds, it was like a light bulb went off in her head for the first time. She realized her husband had truly checked out of their marriage. She could no longer pretend, or be in denial.

Lana had convinced herself, that the only

reason her husband hadn't stopped his cheating ways, was because she never forced the issue. She was under the illusion, she had the authority to put an end to his infidelities if she gave him an ultimatum. Because she assumed there was never a choice, her husband would always choose her. Unfortunately for Lana, the unpleasant truth had erupted in her face, and she was not mentally prepared to handle it.

"You're crazy if you think I would ever give you a divorce. I will be the first, the last, and only Mrs. Mahoney Monroe. Do you hear me!" Lana hollered at the top of her lungs.

"I believe the entire state of Georgia can hear you," Mahoney scoffed. Making no attempt to conceal his disdain for his wife. "Like I previously stated, you have options. Either file for divorce, or stay out my way. But don't question me. Who I see, is none of your business."

"You sonofabitch! How dare you...I'm your fuckin' wife!" Lana's anger and wrath soon turned to gut wrenching pain, as tears swelled up in her eyes. "You can't do this to me...to us, our marriage. You owe me," she wailed.

"I don't owe you anything, but what is stipulated in the postnuptial agreement you willingly signed. Now pull yourself together. Desperation isn't becoming of you."

Mahoney's callous attitude was the final spark that sent Lana on a downward spiral. Any object she could get her hands on, she threw at her husband. It started with her taking off her designer shoes, and it escalated from there—a pricey carved marble sculpture, a one of a kind bronze statue, and then an exquisite Ming Vase.

"You're fuckin' deranged." Mahoney was incensed, but kept his cool. "I'm leaving. I can take my shower someplace else." He disappeared into his closet to pack a few things in a duffel bag, and Lana was right behind him.

"You're not leaving me!" She raged, pounding her fists on her husband's back. Lana then latched her arm around his neck in an attempt to pull him down to the floor. Mahoney swung his body wildly to break his wife's grasp, causing Lana to fly back and hit the wall.

"Don't bother filing divorce papers, because I'll do it for the both of us. My attorney will be on it first thing in the morning. I've been done with you, and now I'm done with this marriage."

"You don't mean that, Mahoney. I'm so sorry. Please don't do this," Lana implored. She had never seen her husband look at her with such repulsion.

"You disgust me." Mahoney stepped over his wife as she laid on the closet floor. He walked over to the nightstand and opened the bottom drawer. He was preoccupied looking for something, that he wasn't paying Lana any attention until he heard her on the phone.

"Help! My husband is trying to kill me!" She yelled into the phone, to the 911 operator, while aiming a gun directly at her husband.

"Lana..." Mahoney reached out his arm to grab the gun out of his wife's hand. But before he could say another word, Lana put three bullets in his chest. She let out one last high pitch cry for help, and then hung up on the operator.

She stood over her husband, watching as he choked on his own blood. Lana knelt down beside him. Life began to leave his body. But she wanted to tell her husband one last thing before he died.

"I hope that toxic bitch was worth losing your life over," Lana whispered in her husband's ear, as he took his very last breath.

Epilogue...

It was a beautiful and rather warm fall day, even for the city of Atlanta. But perfect for tea in the outside garden at the Waldorf Astoria Hotel. Harper sat down and a feeling of calm came over her.

"I was beginning to think you weren't coming," Lana said amusingly, taking a sip of her organic emperor jasmine tea.

"I told you I would be here, and I am." Harper kept her tone polite, but reserved.

"I would think you'd be in a much better mood after receiving my wire transfer this morning," Lana quipped.

"You mean that blood money."

"Keep your voice down," Lana hissed.

"Nobody is here," Harper shot back, glancing around, before continuing. "You told me, you wanted to build a strong case against your husband for infidelity. And having proof he was involved in an ongoing affair with me, would help you secure a better divorce settlement. Never did you mention committing murder. If I knew that was your end game, I would've never agreed to help you."

"Murder was never my intent!" Lana exclaimed. "Besides, the police haven't charged me with murder. I spoke to my attorney this morning. I won't be facing any charges. It's been ruled my husband's unfortunate death, was a case of self-defense."

"Self-defense my ass!"

"Don't you see this black eye." Lana tilted down her sunglasses, revealing her bruised face.

"There is no way Mahoney would've done that to you."

"You're right," Lana giggled. "I actually did it to myself. You have to admit, I did an excellent job," she boasted.

"You are truly a piece of work. Was it always your plan to kill him? Answer me!" Harper demanded to know.

"Calm down. Why the hell do you care anyway. I paid you more money then you will ever see in your pathetic life, just to fuck my husband. You should be grateful."

"I was fucking your husband before you came to me, but you already know this, and it's beside the point. Just answer my question. I have a right to know."

"You lost all your rights when you spread your legs for a married man. But if you must know, I never planned on killing my husband. He drove me to it. It's Mahoney's fault."

"How is it Mahoney's fault, when he's the one that ended up dead. I blame you for his death." Harper proclaimed, pointing her finger directly at Lana.

"If you're looking to blame someone for Mahoney's death, then I suggest you take a long look in the mirror."

"How is it my fault?"

"Like I explained when I came to you with my proposition. You weren't the first woman my husband cheated on me with. You were just one in a long line of many. But..." Lana let out a deep sigh, and put a her head down for a minute.

"But what? Finish what you were saying," Harper pressed.

"But for some sick reason, my husband caught feelings for you." Lana shook her head, still infuriated by that realization. "When I confronted him about his affair with you, he basically told me to either deal with it, or file for divorce. After all those years of being married. We were college sweethearts, and he was willing to throw it away for a cheap tramp like you."

"That's why you killed him, because he didn't want to be with you anymore?"

"NO! I killed him, because I would rather see Mahoney dead, then with you or any other woman," Lana avowed.

Harper wanted to break down and cry, but she was determined to keep her composure. Regret and guilt consumed her mind, and she would never forgive herself. By the time Lana came knocking at her door, Harper was already in love with Mahoney. She should've slammed the door in Lana's face, but her financial offer was way too tempting. Plus, Harper figured it would be a win—win for her. She would take Lana's money, give her all the evidence she needed to get a divorce, which would make Mahoney a free man. They could carry on with their relationship without any worries. Now, the only man Harper ever loved was dead.

"You didn't have to kill him, Lana. Mahoney deserved better than that." A single tear streamed down Harper's cheek.

"Are you crying...you can't be serious," Lana mocked. "I had no idea that heartless hoes had a conscious." She continued with her taunts towards Harper. "By the way, make sure you go pack your shit up, as soon as you leave this table. Now that Mahoney is dead, you will no longer be residing in his condo, because it belongs to me now."

"I won't be packing my belongings, because I'm not going anywhere."

"Excuse me?" Lana raised an eyebrow.

"You heard me. I hate to break it to you. Scratch that, because actually I don't. I'ma need you to share those billions."

"Why in the world would I do that?"

"Because I'm carrying Mahoney Monroe's only heir." Harper proudly announced.

"You lying bitch!" Lana shook the table.

"Nope, it's all true. The reason I was late for tea, is because I had an appointment with my OBGYN. I even brought you a souvenir." Harper reached in her purse and placed the sonogram image on the table in front of Lana.

Lana scrutinized the image, but there was no denying its authenticity. She pushed it away in horror. Knowing the woman who had an affair with her husband, was able to give him the one thing she never could, had Lana ready to commit another murder. This time Harper and the baby she was carrying.

"You won't see a dime of my husband's money. You or that bastard child! I'll tie you up in litigation for so long, you'll be living in a senior citizen facility, before you get your hands on one single dollar. You do not want to go to war with me, you lowdown piece of trash," Lana warned.

"It's hard to go to war, when your locked up in a prison cell for murder."

"Please, like I told you, that case is closed. And if you think anyone is going to take the word of some hired pussy, whose greatest accomplishment is busting it wide open for another woman's husband, over a grieving widow, you're even dumber than I thought. I've wasted enough of my time with the likes of you," she sneered.

Lana took one last sip of tea, stood up and tossed down her napkin ready to go. As she turned to leave, she noticed the two detectives she'd spoken to on the night her husband died, walking towards her.

"I guess this heartless hoe isn't as dumb as you thought," Harper mocked, removing the recording device from underneath her blouse.

"Lana Monroe, turn around and place your hands behind your back." The detective ordered putting the handcuffs on her wrist. "You are under arrest for the murder of Mahoney Monroe."

Your Mommy made it right, Harper said

to herself, placing her hand over her stomach. Knowing Lana would spend the rest of her life in jail for murder wouldn't bring Mahoney back, but it did give Harper the closure she needed, and justice for the unborn child they shared together.

A KING PRODUCTION

All I See Is The Money...

Female
Hustler

A Novel

JOY DEJA KING

Prologue

Nico Carter

"I don't know what you want me to say. I do care about you—"

"But you're still in love with Precious," Lisa said, cutting me off. "I can't deal with this anymore. You're still holding a torch for a woman that has moved on with her life."

"Of course I have love for Precious. We have history and we share a daughter together, but I want to try and make things work with you."

"Oh really, is it because you know Precious has no intentions of leaving her husband or is it because of the baby?"

"Why are you doing this?" I shrugged.

"Doing what... having a real conversation with you? I don't want to be your second choice, or for you to settle for me because of a baby. Nobody even knows about me. I'm a secret. You keep our relationship hidden like you're ashamed of me or something."

"I'm not ashamed of you. With the business I'm in and the lifestyle I'm in, I try to keep my personal life private. I don't want to make you a target."

"Whatever. I used to believe your excuses, but my eyes have been opened. I'm a lot wiser now. I've played my position for so long, believing that my loyalty would prove I was worthy of your love, but I'm done."

"Lisa stop. Why are you crying," I said, reaching for her hand, but she pulled away. "I was always upfront with you. I never sold you a dream."

"You're right. I sold myself a dream. More like a fairytale. But when I heard you on the phone with Precious that fairytale died and reality kicked in."

"What phone conversation?" I asked, hoping Lisa was bluffing.

"The one where you told Precious she and Aaliyah were the loves of your life and nothing would change that, not even the baby you were having with me. It was obvious that was the first time you had ever even mentioned my name to her."

"Lisa, it wasn't like that," I said, stroking my

hand over my face. "You didn't hear or understand the context of the entire conversation." I shook my head; hating Lisa ever heard any of that. "That conversation was over a week ago, why are you just now saying something?"

"Because there was nothing to say. I needed to hear you say those words. I knew what I had to do and I did it."

"So what, you're deciding you don't want to deal with me anymore? It's too late for that. We're having a baby together. You gonna have to deal with me whether you want to or not."

"That's not true."

"Listen, Lisa. I'm sorry you heard what I said to Precious. I know that had to hurt, but again I think you read too much into that. I do care about you."

"Just save it, Nico. You care about me like a puppy," Lisa said sarcastically.

"I get it. Your feelings are hurt and you don't want to have an intimate relationship with me any longer, I have to respect that. But that doesn't change the fact you're carrying my child and I will be playing an active role in their life so I don't want us to be on bad terms. I want to be here for you and our baby."

"You don't have to worry about that anymore. You're free to pursue Precious and not feel obligated to me."

"It's not an obligation. We made the baby together and we'll take care of our child together."

"Don't you get it, there is no baby."

"Excuse me? Are you saying you lied about being pregnant?"

"No, I was pregnant, but…"

"But what, you had a miscarriage?"

"No I had an abortion."

"You killed my child?"

"No, I aborted mine!"

"That was my child, too."

"Fuck you! Fuck you, Nico! You want to stand there and act like you gave a damn about our baby and me. You're such a hypocrite and a liar."

"You had no right to make a decision like that without discussing it with me."

"I had every right. I heard you on the phone confessing your love to another woman and the child you all share together. Making it seem like our baby and me was some unwanted burden. Well now you no longer have that burden. Any child I bring into this world deserves better than that."

"You killed my child because of a phone conversation you overheard. You make me sick. I think I actually hate you."

"Now you know how I feel because I hate you too," Lisa spit back with venom in her voice.

"You need to go before you meet the same demise as the baby you murdered."

"No worries, I have no intentions of staying. As a matter of fact, I came to say goodbye. I have no reason to stay in New York."

"You're leaving town?"

"Yes, for good. Like I said, there is nothing here for me. I don't want to be in the same city as you. It would be a constant reminder of all the time I wasted waiting for you," Lisa said, as a single tear trickled down her cheek. "Goodbye, Nico."

I watched with contempt and pain as Lisa walked out the door. I couldn't lie to myself. I almost understood why she chose not to keep our baby. I wasn't in love with Lisa and couldn't see me spending the rest of my life with her. The fucked up part was it had nothing to do with her. Lisa was a good girl, but she was right, my heart still belonged to Precious. But I still hated her for aborting our baby. I guess that made me a selfish man. I wanted Lisa to bless me with another child that I could be a father to, but have her accept that she would never have my heart.

At this moment, it was all insignificant. That chapter was now closed. Lisa was out of my life. In the process, she took our child with her and for that I would never forgive her.

Seven Months Later...

"Look at her, mommy, she is so beautiful," Lisa said, holding her newborn daughter in the hospital.

"She is beautiful," her mother said, nodding her head. "What are you going to name her?"

"Angel. She's my little Angel." Lisa smiled.

"That's a beautiful name and she is an angel," Lisa's mother said, admiring her granddaughter. "Lisa, are you okay?" she asked, noticing her daughter becoming pale with a pain stricken expression on her face.

"I'm getting a headache, but I'll be fine," Lisa said, trying to shake off the discomfort. "Can you hold Angel for a minute. I need to sit up and catch my breath," Lisa said, handing her baby to her mother.

"I would love to." Her mother smiled, gently rocking Angel.

"I feel a little nauseated," Lisa said, feeling hot.

"Do you want me to get the nurse?"

"No, just get me some water," Lisa said. Before Lisa's mother even had a chance to reach for a bottle of water, her daughter began to vomit. In a matter of seconds Lisa's arms and legs began jerking. Her entire body seemed to be having convulsions."

"Lisa... Lisa... what's the matter baby!" Lisa's mother said, her voice shaking, filled with fear. "Somebody get a doctor!" she screamed out, running to the door and holding her grandbaby close to her chest. "My daughter needs a doctor. She's sick! Somebody help her please!" she pleaded, yelling out as she held the door wide open.

"Ma'am, please step outside," a nurse said,

rushing into Lisa's room with a couple of other nurses behind her and the doctor close behind.

Lisa's mother paced back and forth in front of her daughter's room for what seemed like an eternity. "It's gonna be okay, Angel. Your mother will be fine," she kept saying over and over again to her grandbaby. "You know they say babies are healing, and you healing your grandmother's soul right now," she said softly in Angel's ear.

"Ma'am."

"Yes... is my daughter okay?" she asked rushing towards the doctor.

"Ma'am, your daughter was unconscious then her heart stopped."

"What are you saying?" she questioned as her bottom lip began trembling.

"We did everything we could do, but your daughter didn't make it. I'm sorry."

"No! No! She's so young. She's just a baby herself. How did this happen?"

"I'm not sure, but we're going to do an autopsy. It will take a couple of weeks for the results to get back. It could be a placental abruption and amniotic fluid embolism, or a brain aneurysm, we don't know. Again, I'm sorry. Do you want us to contact the father of your granddaughter?" the doctor asked.

Lisa's mother gazed down at Angel, whose eyes were closed as she slept peacefully in her arms. "I don't know who Angel's father is. That information died with my daughter."

"I understand. Again, I'm sorry about your daughter. Let us know if there is anything we can do for you," the doctor said before walking off.

"I just want to see my daughter and tell her goodbye," she said walking into Lisa's room. "My sweet baby girl. You look so peaceful." Lisa's mother rubbed her hand across the side of her face. "Don't you worry. I promise I will take care of Angel. I will give her all the love I know you would have. Rest in peace baby girl."

Coming Soon

A KING PRODUCTION

All I See Is The Money...

Female Hustler 7

A Novel

JOY DEJA KING

Read The Entire Bitch Series in This Order

PAUSE...NOW LET ME SPEAK

Join us on the
Clubhouse app
Every Wednesday @6pm EST

Toxic *Relationships...How*
Should You Deal With Them?

Hosted by:

Miss P

Instagram: misstp90
Twitter: misstp90
Facebook: MissPtv

Kevin Elliott
"Instagram authorkelliott"

Joy Deja King

Facebook: Joy "Deja" King
Website: joydejaking.com

Blake Karrington

P.O. Box 912
Collierville, TN 38027

A KING PRODUCTION

www.joydejaking.com
www.twitter.com/joydejaking

ORDER FORM

Name:

Address:

City/State:

Zip:

QUANTITY	TITLES	PRICE	TOTAL
	Bitch	$15.00	
	Bitch Reloaded	$15.00	
	The Bitch Is Back	$15.00	
	Queen Bitch	$15.00	
	Last Bitch Standing	$15.00	
	Superstar	$15.00	
	Ride Wit' Me	$12.00	
	Ride Wit' Me Part 2	$15.00	
	Stackin' Paper	$15.00	
	Trife Life To Lavish	$15.00	
	Trife Life To Lavish II	$15.00	
	Stackin' Paper II	$15.00	
	Rich or Famous	$15.00	
	Rich or Famous Part 2	$15.00	
	Rich or Famous Part 3	$15.00	
	Bitch A New Beginning	$15.00	
	Mafia Princess Part 1	$15.00	
	Mafia Princess Part 2	$15.00	
	Mafia Princess Part 3	$15.00	
	Mafia Princess Part 4	$15.00	
	Mafia Princess Part 5	$15.00	
	Boss Bitch	$15.00	
	Baller Bitches Vol. 1	$15.00	
	Baller Bitches Vol. 2	$15.00	
	Baller Bitches Vol. 3	$15.00	
	Bad Bitch	$15.00	
	Still The Baddest Bitch	$15.00	
	Power	$15.00	
	Power Part 2	$15.00	
	Drake	$15.00	
	Drake Part 2	$15.00	
	Female Hustler	$15.00	
	Female Hustler Part 2	$15.00	
	Female Hustler Part 3	$15.00	
	Female Hustler Part 4	$15.00	
	Female Hustler Part 5	$15.00	
	Female Hustler Part 6	$15.00	
	Princess Fever "Birthday Bash"	$6.00	
	Nico Carter The Men Of The Bitch Series	$15.00	
	Bitch The Beginning Of The End	$15.00	
	Supreme...Men Of The Bitch Series	$15.00	
	Bitch The Final Chapter	$15.00	
	Stackin' Paper III	$15.00	
	Men Of The Bitch Series And The Women Who Love Them	$15.00	
	Coke Like The 80s	$15.00	
	Baller Bitches The Reunion Vol. 4	$15.00	
	Stackin' Paper IV	$15.00	
	The Legacy	$15.00	
	Lovin' Thy Enemy	$15.00	
	Stackin' Paper V	$15.00	
	The Legacy Part 2	$15.00	
	Assassins - Episode 1	$11.00	
	Assassins - Episode 2	$11.00	
	Assassins - Episode 2	$11.00	
	Bitch Chronicles	$40.00	
	So Hood So Rich	$15.00	
	Stackin' Paper VI	$15.00	
	Female Hustler Part 7	$15.00	
	Toxic...	$6.00	

Shipping/Handling (Via Priority Mail) $7.50 1-2 Books, $15.00 3-4 Books add $1.95 for ea. **Additional book.**
Total: $_____FORMS OF ACCEPTED PAYMENTS: Certified or government issued checks and money Orders, all mail in orders take 5-7 Business days to be delivered

CPSIA information can be obtained
at www.ICGtesting.com
Printed in the USA
LVHW031034200322
713908LV00003B/556